Underwater

Written by
Karen Hoenecke

Illustrated by
Andrea Tachiera

Down, down deep to the ocean floor.
You can see rocks and caves
and so much more!

There are orange fish, striped fish,
black fish, and blue.

3

There are starfish, jellyfish,

and prickly fish, too.

There are sponges, snails,

and fish with long tails.

Some fish have a light.

Some fish like to bite.

Some fish wear a frown.

Some swim upside down.

11

Some fish take a nap.

Some fish set a trap.

There are ships buried deep…

and the secrets they keep.

Down, down deep to the ocean floor.
You can see rocks and caves
and so much more!